Archie and the Bear

For Rosie, in her bear suit—**ZL**

For William Venturini, the capo—**DM**

Little Hare Books
an imprint of
Hardie Grant Egmont
Ground Floor, Building 1, 658 Church Street
Richmond, Victoria 3121, Australia

www.littleharebooks.com

Designed and lettered by David Mackintosh
The illustrations in this book were made using pen,
pencil, ink, watercolour and kraft paper.

First published 2017

Cataloguing-in-Publication details are available
from the National Library of Australia

978 1 760127 51 0 (hbk.)

This book was edited by
Margrete Lamond and Alyson O'Brien
Production management by Sally Davis
Produced by Pica Digital, Singapore
Printed through Asia Pacific Offset
Printed in Shenzhen, Guangdong Province, China

54321

Archie and the Bear

zanni louise

david mackintosh

LITTLE 🐇 HARE

www.littleharebooks.com

Archie was a bear.

But everywhere Archie went, people
patted him on the head and said,
'I like your bear suit.'

'It's NOT a suit,'
Archie would growl.
'I AM a bear!'

One day, Archie had had enough.
He packed his bear sack
and set off for the forest.

Archie walked and stumbled
and walked.

He rested against a tree
and nibbled his honey sandwich.

By afternoon,
the forest
grew dark.

Archie knew
bears shouldn't
be scared, so he
kept walking
and sharpened
his bear eyes.

Just then,
a bear appeared.

'Argh!'
cried
Archie.

'Hello,' said the bear.

When Archie realised the bear was friendly, he said, 'I like your boy suit.'

'It's NOT a suit,' growled the bear. 'I AM a boy!'

The bear was clearly not a boy. But Archie didn't want to hurt the bear's feelings.

'Would you like a
honey sandwich?'
asked Archie.

The bear smiled and took a bite.

'Boys like sandwiches,' he said.

'Bears like honey,'
said Archie.

Archie and the bear walked along the river.

The bear showed Archie how to skim stones across the water.

Archie was very good at skimming stones.

Archie showed the bear how
to catch fish with his claw.

The bear was very
good at catching fish.

The bear showed
Archie how to read.

Archie read to the bear.

Archie showed the bear how to scoop honey from the log.

The bear scooped honey out for Archie.

As night
deepened,
the forest
cooled.

The bear
shivered.

'Would you like to wear my
bear suit?' asked Archie.
'Yes, please,' said the bear.

Archie undressed.
Then he too shivered.

The bear took off his boy jumper
and gave it to Archie.
But still, they were cold.

'Do boys like warm quilts?' asked
Archie. 'I have a very warm one
where I live.'

The bear nodded,
so Archie led the bear home.

They pulled the warm quilt
around them and nibbled honey
sandwiches next to the fire.

'Boys like warm quilts
and warm fire,' said the bear.

'So do bears,' said Archie.